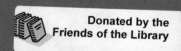

Lucy and the Bully

by Claire Alexander

Albert Whitman & Company
Morton Grove, Illinois

For Dennis, Christine, Mark, Elsie, and Jim . . .
C.A.

Library of Congress Cataloging-in-Publication Data

Alexander, Claire.
Lucy and the bully / written and illustrated by Claire Alexander.
p. cm.
Summary: When a mean classmate in preschool wrecks Lucy's artwork,
she discovers that they can be friends once he stops being jealous of her.
ISBN 978-0-8075-4786-1
[1. Bullies—Fiction. 2. Nursery schools—Fiction. 3. Schools—Fiction. 4. Animals—Fiction.] I. Title.
PZ7.A37666Lu 2008 [E]—dc22 2008001340

First published in Great Britain in 2008 by Gullane Children's Books.

For more information about Albert Whitman & Company, visit our web site at www.albertwhitman.com.

NOTE TO PARENTS AND TEACHERS

Children need the guidance of caring adults. With bullying, as in most of life's challenges, young children need our guidance most. Bullying is the use of aggressive, intentional, and often repetitive behavior in order to exert power over another person. A bullied child feels defenseless and intimidated; he or she may be uncertain about seeking help. The child should be encouraged to seek help from an adult as soon as possible, rather than attempt to "work it out" with a bully. He or she should also never be made to feel solely responsible for ending the bullying.

The harmful effects of bullying can be lessened greatly when we are available, accessible, and attuned to all children in our care. We need to find a way to talk with children about bullying early, as soon as children have the language to describe what they witness and experience.

Because children learn by example, sharing stories of bullying situations with successful resolutions can provide children with good information about bullying—and about themselves. It allows them to imagine similar scenarios and consider how they might act. Reading such stories with children—as much as the stories themselves—creates a safe connection between caretakers and children. Sharing stories addresses a difficult topic and strengthens a feeling of safety, so it can be a powerful act of love. This connection, this feeling, and this act are the best protectors against bullies.

Daniel G. Gill, M.S.M.F.T., L.C.P.C.
Staff Therapist at The Family Institute at Northwestern University
Evanston, Illinois

At school, everyone wanted
Lucy to draw for them.

"You are so good at drawing, Lucy."

"Can you please draw me a picture of a rabbit, Lucy?"

Well, not *quite* everyone . . .

Tommy went over to Lucy's table.
"Oops," he said, as he pushed over the paint.
He didn't look sorry.

"Oh, dear!" cried Ms. Goosie.
"Accidents will happen.
Let's get this mess cleaned up!"

The next day everyone made clay models.
Ms. Goosie gave Lucy a gold star for her blackbird.

Pig
by
Tyler

Worm
by
Hannah

Monster
by
Ethan

(Even though Ms. Goosie thought it was a crow.)

After school, Lucy carried her model very carefully so it wouldn't break.

Tommy was waiting for her.

"Let's see your stupid crow!" he said.
"It's . . . it's a blackbird," Lucy stammered.
But Tommy grabbed it, and then . . .

Lucy put her broken blackbird
in her bag so her mother
wouldn't see. And she
didn't say anything.

That night, Lucy tried hard to put her blackbird
back together, but it didn't look the same.
"What happened to your model?" her mother asked.
"I . . . I dropped it," said Lucy.

Over the next week, Lucy's mother wondered what was wrong.

On Monday,
Lucy brought home a
ripped storybook.

On Tuesday,
she brought home
a crumpled painting,

and on Wednesday,
all her pencils
were broken.

Lucy looked sadder and sadder every day,
but she wouldn't tell her mother why.

On Thursday, Lucy brought
home a cake she'd made at school.
"Who put a hoofprint in the
middle of it?" her mother asked.
"I . . . I don't know," said Lucy.

But at last she said,
"It was Tommy."

"Don't worry, Honey, I'll take care of this," Lucy's mother said.
She picked up the telephone.
"May I speak to Ms. Goosie, please?" she asked.
"No, Mommy," Lucy wailed.
"Please don't tell Ms. Goosie!"

But it was too late.

That night, Lucy couldn't sleep.
She was afraid of what would happen the next day.

In the morning, Lucy
didn't want to go to school.
"Don't worry.
It will be okay,"
said her mother.

Tommy didn't want
to go to school, either.

At story time, Tommy was very quiet.

At play time Tommy looked
very alone and very sad.
Lucy wasn't scared of him anymore.
(She even felt a little sorry for him.)

At art time, Lucy saw Tommy drawing. He was
drawing a porcupine, and it was a very good porcupine.
Its spines looked very sharp and spiky indeed.

Lucy decided to tell him exactly
what she thought of it.

"I like your porcupine, Tommy," Lucy said.
"It's not a porcupine. It's a hedgehog," said Tommy.
"Well, it's very good," said Lucy. "Could you draw one for me, too?"

Tommy was surprised.
No one had ever asked him to draw anything before.

"You can have this one," said Tommy.
"Thank you, Tommy," said Lucy.

"I'm sorry I was mean, and did all those things,
and most of all I'm sorry I stomped on your crow," Tommy said.
"It was a very good crow."

"I forgive you, Tommy,"
said Lucy. "But it wasn't
a crow, it was a blackbird."

They both laughed.
And then they went
outside to play.